COLOURS OF THE SEA

Also by Guy Hall

Our Vietnam

Coming Next

Taste of Earth
Scent of Heaven
Touch of Eternity

Guy Hall

COLOURS OF THE SEA

Illustrations
by
Meredith Hall

TINY FISH PUBLISHING

To new beginnings.

The feeling of being 'okay'
doesn't imply
that you have risen above
all your faults
and all your fears.

It simply implies
that you refuse
to be paralysed by them.

Anonymous

'The voice of the sea speaks to the soul.'

Kate Chopin

CONTENTS

AUSTRALIA
BRISBANE
PORT STEPHENS
SYDNEY
MELBOURNE
N
W
E
S

NEW
CALEDONIA

NORFOLK
ISLAND

TO
TUVALU
TO
PITCAIRN
ISLAND
AUCKLAND
NEW
ZEALAND

Voyage Log.

18 March 1999

0720:   *Cast off from Nelson Bay,*
       wind NNW 8-10 kts,
       clear skies.

       Boat sound. Comms good.

       Underway! Can't wait... MSC

Those who know the sea know. There are those who fear her, and there are those who respect her, deeply. More often than not, respect is won through adversity. Respect for the sea is no different. She has challenged many. She has hurt many. It is those who return, no grudges borne, who learn to respect, then to love.

'Maddie' Spencer Christian knew the sea. 'It's in your blood,' she had been told. 'Too many times!' she'd often thought. Raised in a remote and sometimes wild corner of the South Pacific Ocean, Maddie could see, smell, and hear the sea every waking moment. To her, the sea was as much a part of life as breathing itself. But like breathing itself, she knew that all too often she had taken it for granted. She hadn't meant to. It had just happened like that.

She was a seventh-generation Norfolk Islander. If she wanted to, she could trace her ancestry back to Fletcher Christian himself – in all his glory, or infamy, depending on who was asking. Her family had lived on the island for nearly one hundred and fifty years, and for more than half a century before that on an even smaller island called 'Pitcairn'. For all those years, and all those generations, the sea had surrounded them, had nurtured them – was part of them. She had fished since she was five. She had canoed, then sailed, since she was nine. Her ancestry was the sea. Her teacher was the sea. Her comfort was the sea.

'Yes, was...' she mused, as she mentally shrugged off all the years since leaving her island home for the siren call of a career, another island, and another world. As the bow of her sloop, *The Lady Jane*, sliced its way through the moderate swell, carefully casting aside the spray it created with each strike of each wave, she gazed skyward and soaked up the warm sun, together with the memories that eased their way back into her consciousness.

High above her, a jet airliner – from Sydney, she supposed – cut its own way through the cold, rarefied air, its four powerful turbofan engines pushing it along effortlessly close to the speed of sound. At odds with that tremendous power were the delicate contrails behind each engine, the four merging into one long, thin, celestial footprint of the sleek and comfortable craft to which they belonged. A technological marvel with a cloud as a footprint! She liked that.

It was from such a sleek and comfortable craft that she had gazed down onto where she was now, and suddenly, emotionally, and almost reluctantly realised that she had been gone too long. The young flight attendant had seen her looking down, a world away. 'Imagine being down there!' she had joked, her blue eyes twinkling as she enthusiastically endorsed the wonder of flight. 'Yes, imagine that...' Maddie had replied, and she knew. She had to do it again.

So here she was. A doctor, a specialist, a successful scientist, sailing solo from Australia to

Norfolk Island, just as she had done when she was eighteen years old. But now, she was 'a little over' forty. She had accomplished all that she had wanted to. Medical degree, oncologist, research fellow. She had sat on the boards of institutions that had pushed the boundaries of cancer research further than anyone had ever dreamed possible. And successes had come with it. They were closer than ever before. Hopes were high. Expectations were even higher. A bright and extraordinary future beckoned her on, urging her to greater and more wonderful things.

So why did she feel so empty, so unfulfilled? In truth, not a single life had truly been saved. Prolonged, maybe, but not saved. When she left the island, she knew exactly what her goals were, and she knew exactly how to achieve them. At least, how to get started. One of the marvelous things about youth is the clarity of its optimism. 'And so it should be,' she reflected. Maturity tends to cloud many things. Because now – from the 'other side' – everything was different. It was like looking at someone with the sun setting on their face: their skin alight, their eyes reflecting the fiery glow, full of life, then slowly walking around behind them and seeing nothing but shadow, a silhouette against a fading light.

Sunsets were one of Maddie's great loves. Night after night as a child, she had sat on the porch of her parents' house and watched the blazing sun sink slowly into the darkening sea, setting the waves on fire, but the water inevitably, and inexorably, extinguishing its mighty glow. They were among the few things in life that she never grew tired of. There was something inherently reassuring about them. Despite being the end of the day, and the herald of night – with all its darkness and dreams – to Maddie they were the quiet promise of a new tomorrow.

The airliner had disappeared into the distance now. Its contrail, too, was slowly being dispersed by an obviously powerful but changing wind aloft. On the surface, the breeze was shifting too – 'backing' a little – the steady north-easterly becoming a freshening northerly. As she glanced over her shoulder, she could see high prefrontal cloud streaming out from the western horizon, the afternoon light catching its eastern edge and giving it a golden glow. Further west though, and closer to the horizon, a uniform curtain of grey merged into the sea. Very soon, that grey curtain would glow red with this day's setting sun.

Maddie moved forward and eased the jib a little to accommodate the changing wind, then went below to check the latest weather via the 'Sat-link'. The weather system she could see behind her, and had known of since leaving Port Stephens, had slipped off the east coast and was steadily moving eastward at thirty knots – fast for a front at this time of year, and faster than at first predicted. Now, crowding up against the high-pressure system centred in the southern Tasman Sea, the prefrontal northerlies were forecast to exceed forty-five knots. Maddie leaned over her plotting chart and pursed her lips.

At its current speed, the front would overtake her in about thirty hours. If she could maintain an average of eight knots… given that she could probably run with spinnaker as the wind turned further to the northwest… the weather was going to catch her, and… yes… things might get a 'little exciting' about fifty nautical miles to run to Norfolk. She mentally assessed her options, imagining the sea state, the wind conditions, and the distance to sail. She pictured a rising and furious sea; rolling waves looming above her as *The Lady Jane* met the challenge of the storm, plunging into the wavefronts, being lifted by the swell and pitching off the churning tops. Images of the recent 1998 Sydney to Hobart yacht race came back to her: of eighty-foot waves, of boats being rolled not once, but three times, before surrendering and breaking up before the might of that maelstrom. A freak storm. Nothing else. She wondered…

She mentally, then physically, shrugged, then paused again, thoughtful. Was there doubt there? Even fear? Either was okay, she told herself. Both healthy, in their own way. What she didn't feel was helpless. She knew her skills, and more importantly, she knew her limitations. Moreover, she knew her boat's limitations. Decision-making had never been hard for her – just living with those decisions, sometimes.

She returned to the cockpit at the stern. With the aid of the freshening breeze, *The Lady Jane* was strongly slicing her way through the darkening sea. She relaxed a little. Cooler now, too. She shivered. Reaching into the locker next to the steering wheel, she slipped into her lined spray jacket, zipping it up to her chin. Then, settling into the padded seat behind the helm, steadily holding its course, Maddie thought of her mother.

Even when Maddie had left Norfolk Island for Sydney, to begin her studies, she knew of her mother's condition. So cruel that the same spectre that had stolen her father this time loomed over her mother. Maddie's departure from Norfolk was coloured with a greater determination than ever to make a difference. Seven years later, as a newly registered Doctor of Medicine, an intern at Sydney's Royal North Shore Hospital, she had sat beside her mother's bed holding a hand that so many times had gently and lovingly held hers. At that moment, in all her triumph, in all her celebration, with her newfound and hard-earned knowledge, she had never felt more helpless or more useless in her entire life.

She had flown her mother back to Norfolk and laid her next to the man who was 'her life'. From high on Mount Pitt, Maddie had watched the most gut-wrenching sunset of her young life. Long after the water had turned inky black, and the island had fallen quiet, her tears flowed, as she stared towards a dark horizon and let the sea comfort her. She flew to Sydney the very next day and left her island home behind. Her subsequent visits became just that – visits – into her past, and into sorrows she could not fathom.

The eastern horizon was now fading with the coming of night. She breathed in the salt air and managed a smile. Perhaps Tahu was right all along. 'You'll come back when you are ready; when it is right.' She could see his round, smiling face, his tight black curls, his broad Polynesian nose, and his beautiful white teeth. Yes, she was coming home. And maybe, after all, it wasn't because she had 'achieved nothing'. Maybe she had achieved all that she needed to, in order to return home, to nurture the island and the islanders she loved.

"Dear Tahu," she said aloud. "Will you remember me..?"

She smiled again, recollecting. "Will you even be there?" And her smile waned just a little.

Tahu was quite literally the boy next door. He was the adopted son of one of Norfolk's greatest and most trusted elders. Laurence, a 'weatherman' by trade, had fished and sailed the waters around Norfolk Island nearly all his adult life, except for the time he had spent on Tuvalu, doing exactly the same thing. Tahu's natural parents were something of a mystery, to Maddie anyway. Tahu never spoke of them much. The only times he had, she had learned that he didn't know much about them either, other than that his mother was a Tuvaluan islander and his father a French missionary.

Laurence regularly took children from the orphanage fishing and sailing. Tahu and he were instantly captivated by each other. The sisters had said that Tahu had never smiled as much as he did at this enigmatic, slightly greying meteorologist-turned-fisherman. He had given this bright young islander new joy, a new life. It was not difficult to make the necessary arrangements. Before long, Tahu gave Laurence a new life, too, as a father, as a hero, and as a confidant – his greatest friend. Leaving Tuvalu was difficult for both of them. But, like the sea, life goes on.

Physically, Tahu was one of the most amazing people Maddie had ever known. He was tall and strong, with typically 'milk chocolate' skin, and close, black curly hair. While his skin was somewhat paler than the average, his features were those of a Tuvaluan, and he carried them proudly. His eyes, on the other hand, seemed to tell another story. Calm and calming. 'Touched by God,' some had said. To Maddie, however, they echoed something else – for Tahu had different coloured eyes. One blue, one green. 'The colours of the sea', she had often thought. And how he loved the sea! But those different hues reflected another and, to her, a sometimes-hypnotising side of his nature. He was, in many ways, the most objective person she had ever known. He could always see both sides of an issue, a circumstance, or a person. One blue, one green. He could, at once, be clinically sure that everything would be all right, but at the same time know just what to say to someone who was not so sure.

Tahu had come to the island when he was ten years old, and she eleven. Laurence had been gone for nearly two years, and his return brought new joy to Maddie. Her own father had died whilst he was away, and although Laurence was there for James' funeral, he had soon returned to Tuvalu. His coming home to Norfolk opened a new and wonderful chapter in Maddie's youth.

Maddie and Tahu became not only sailing and fishing companions, but companions. They grew, and fought, and made up, most of the time. Laurence would sit and watch them fishing, or cleaning the boats, or sitting on his porch at sunset and, although not a great one for emotion, he sometimes found things getting just a tiny bit blurry and his throat becoming tight. He knew that Maddie's mother, Anne, felt the same. Though 'only children', they found in each other, and each other's parent, comfort and surety. Nothing too sentimental, just surety. And that was good.

At sixteen and seventeen respectively, there was that one time when Tahu tried to say something, about something else, but even he had little idea what he was trying to say. Maddie smiled and tucked her chin into her spray jacket as she remembered what in many ways was the sweetest moment of her youth on Norfolk Island – holding hands with this tall, strapping young islander, neither saying a word, as they gazed out to sea, feeling like nothing could ever be better than 'this'.

And for a time, an important time, that was the closest they ever got in that respect. It was almost as if their friendship wouldn't allow 'love' into their world, as if friendship was jealous of what love might bring, or change. So, they stayed friends, the very best of friends. But love is persistent. And friendship is many things. When she left for the world of healing, and he for the world of the sea, their changing and ever-deepening love was left behind, but not forgotten. Far from forgotten...

He had studied Oceanography and Climate at the University of Auckland. He had spent time on Tuvalu, as well as on many of the other islands in the South Pacific. But she remembered hearing that he still based himself out of Norfolk Island. Tahu loved Norfolk. It was very different from the island of his birth, but it had become his home. It was where Laurence was. But despite that, his passion was still Tuvalu.

The small island nation of Tuvalu, it seemed, was destined to be among the first victims of the phenomenon being labelled 'global warming'. As one of the lowest-lying countries in the world, and with forecasts of rising sea levels and more frequent and wild storms, Tuvalu's destiny was at best uncertain, at worst unimaginable. Already as a result of storms in 1997, one of her smaller islands had virtually ceased to exist – swept into the sea – leaving behind nothing but a forlorn, sandy knoll.

But Tahu was anything but fatalistic about Tuvalu's future. 'Whilst there is light, there is hope,' he would remind himself as he resolutely and methodically tackled the enormous task he had undertaken. Its enormity did not bother him. He had viewed the problem from every angle, yet was always looking for new perspectives. He had travelled widely in search of the key to the puzzle, the elusive clue, the embryo of a solution. From

Sydney to San Francisco, from Alaska to the tip of South America, he had visited all corners of the Pacific. 'The answer is there, somewhere. We just have to find it.'

To deal with a problem, one had to look elsewhere, he had said, as he expounded his cutting-edge thinking about El Nino, La Nina and the warming and cooling of the Pacific currents. 'Much like medicine,' she had agreed. To treat a symptom was not to treat the cause. And symptoms could often be misleading of the cause...

"And not just in medicine...," she murmured as she flicked the switch on the stern control panel to illuminate her running and navigation lights. The night would be a good one for speed, and hence distance, in front of the weather chasing her from behind.

"But eventually," he had said as he draped his toe in the water beneath 'the raft', as it gently bobbed in the idyllic, crystal waters of Emily Bay, "Eventually, you have to return to where you started from, to complete your work."

"But Tahu," she laughed, "you can't save Tuvalu by sitting on the sand and doing a King Canute! It doesn't matter how knowledgeable you are! Whether it be medicine or sea levels, coming home to nobly face defeat will do nothing for your cause. Your island will still sink. People will still die." And she bit into her lip as the tears burned behind her eyes.

"You miss the point, Maddie. I didn't say anything about facing defeat. Or winning, for that matter." He looked out towards Phillip Island and smiled. "At some point, Maddie, your work is complete. And you have to come home."

And he was right. The first stars were slowly brightening in the deep azure sky above her, and she no longer felt quite so empty. She was coming 'home', whether her 'work' was complete or not.

So? Now...? Again, she wondered. This time, she reproached herself at the thought. Too long. Too little contact. Even if he was there.

"Typical!" she muttered as the descending darkness threatened to bring her mood down with it. "So focused on your own life and 'life goals', you forgot to keep on living..." Not anymore, though. Tahu was right, whether he was there or not!

Tahu was right on so many occasions. That was what was so amazing about him. At times, it seemed that he didn't have a single irrational bone in his body – much to Maddie's disgust! But deep down, she found great comfort there.

Like the time she had been having a 'really bad' day. It was her father's anniversary. Her mother's condition was serious, and she had been given 'only months', but of course, 'they couldn't be sure.' Although she couldn't see it at the time, Maddie realised, later, that she was probably making the day even harder for herself. She wasn't quite wallowing in self-pity, but she was certainly feeling very sorry for herself. It was one of the few times she could remember that Tahu had genuinely chastised her.

They were back on Norfolk, as they routinely were, both on breaks from their studies. She was twenty-six and nearing the end of her studies. He was twenty-five and already rapidly gaining recognition as a gifted and tireless warrior in the fight to better understand the planet. But true to his nature, he was ever the realist. He didn't harbour any dreams of miraculously reversing sea levels or of somehow speeding up the patching of the ozone layer. His goal was to learn, to anticipate, and then maybe, just maybe, make a difference. He was patient.

On this day, however, such things were far away. Maddie was struggling, like never before. But true to her nature, she was fighting. Her heart was full of sorrow, but her pale grey eyes were full of fire.

"Maddie, Maddie… I know it's tough," he said softly, "but please, please don't…"

"Tahu," she whispered, "as a ten-year-old kid, I watched my father literally fade away. I so much wanted to be able to do something, anything, to make him feel better. But I couldn't. I was so angry. And I was so sad. I…" She swallowed hard, desperately trying to keep her composure. "I loved him so much, Tahu. And I couldn't help him!"

"Maddie, I understand. I know how you loved him."

"No! Tahu, you don't understand! You haven't watched both your parents die. You don't know what it is like!"

"I do, Maddie…"

"Tahu, you don't!" she said, shaking her head.

"You forget Maddie. I have no parents either…"

"But Tahu," she gasped, "Laurence…"

"Laurence!" he snapped and then hesitated, as though the words that were coming suddenly got all jumbled together and caught in his throat; as if, while his lips were still forming them, they never arrived. "Laurence!" he gasped. "Laurence," he finally whispered, "is not my father. He is the greatest, the most wonderful part… the very centre of my life. He is my anchor, Maddie. I love him. But he is not my real father."

"Tahu…"

"Maddie! No! You listen to me now! I know that you are hurting. But don't you see? That your parents have both suffered from the same condition shouldn't be your motivation for finding a cure! Surely, surely, Maddie, your motivation is to save someone else's parents from the same fate. I know it must be Maddie. Tell me it is!"

"Tahu, of course it is! Medicine is my life, my vocation. But I feel I owe them this. If I can do this, I must."

"You must, eh?" he said, almost under his breath. He turned and looked away. "You know, Maddie," he said haltingly, "sometimes it doesn't matter what I say to you, I cannot reach you. I just cannot reach you!"

"Oh, Tahu Taleka," she said softly as she stepped closer to him and wiped a single tear from his dark cheek. "I'm sorry. It's easy. Just keep being my friend," and looking up at him, she gave him a genuinely sheepish and disarming smile.

Tahu said nothing. Instead, he opened his arms wide and allowed her to step closer still. As his arms closed around her, she gently rested her cheek against his chest, and sobbed as though her heart would break.

He was not there at her mother's funeral five months later, although Laurence, again, was. Tahu was on a research ship, in the Antarctic of all places. He had sent her a message of support. It was in Tuvaluan – his code to her that it came from the deepest place in his heart.

By the time Maddie had curled up in her bunk and strapped herself in, she was feeling better. Memories of her parents, of Tahu, and of the waters she knew so well had eased her anxiety and, even if she said so herself, she was feeling very much at ease. Confident that she was doing what she wanted to do, Maddie Spencer Christian was happy.

Twenty-four hours later, however, Maddie's mood was a little different.

She had awoken, at dawn, to a blazing red sky. 'Sailor's warning...' she had murmured offhandedly as she crept her way towards the stern with a coffee in her hand and settled back into the padded cockpit seat to take full advantage of the extraordinary panorama emerging around her.

Overnight, the almost translucent blue skies of the day before had surrendered to a delicate yet solid dome of rippled, high-altitude, cirrus cloud. Though still concealed behind the eastern horizon, the daybreak sun was already flooding that dome with a vivid scarlet flush. The intense, glittering, sapphire blue of the sea surface had darkened to a sombre steel grey, flecked with gold. As the swell lengthened and the wave tops pushed higher, the ocean began to heave and sigh, flinging sheets of spray into the early dawn light. As she had done throughout the night, *The Lady Jane* continued to reliably and capably cut her way onwards. But the gentle, rhythmic slosh of water against the bow was now being interrupted sporadically by the harsher slap of increasingly agitated waves. Hurried along by the strengthening breeze, foamy wind lanes snaked out to the horizon, hissing past the boat and whispering a warning she could not ignore.

From the stern, she had looked for'ard, past the mast and mainsail, past the foresail, taut and eager in the wind, and past the bow lancing its way onwards towards her destination. Remote and beautiful Norfolk Island was her birthplace – her spiritual home – and her skin prickled at the thought of being back on its rugged, basaltic shores. But on this dramatic and brilliant morning, it lay well beyond the ever-brightening horizon, still well beyond her reach.

As the sun rose higher and the scarlet dome faded to grey, she contemplated the nearly four kilometres of water beneath her – cold, dark, and quiet. Yet, powerful beyond measure. Far below her tiny vessel, in the very heart of the ocean, massive upwelling currents transported the Earth's energy and shaped its complex and constantly changing climate. And yet, most of the ocean remained unexplored. Scientists knew more about the most distant planets in the solar system, and the vast realms of space beyond, than they knew about the boundless oceans that cocoon most of the Earth. To travel to the floor of the ocean, to glimpse into its deepest and darkest recesses, to explore just a fraction of its might, presents almost insurmountable challenges.

Water is dense. It absorbs light. Even metres below the surface, colours change, then disappear. The first to go is red. The last are blue and green. Just two hundred metres down, the remaining light from above begins to fade. At a depth of one thousand meters, sunlight is essentially absent, and the ocean enters the aphotic, or midnight zone, where it is perpetually dark.

Water is heavy. Just ten metres below the sea surface, the pressure of the water is already double that of the atmosphere at the surface. At the edge of the midnight zone, the weight of the water above exerts a pressure one hundred times that of the surface. And at the sandy sea floor, four thousand metres beneath her, Maddie knew that the pressure was equivalent to nearly four hundred atmospheres. Without specialised equipment, and nerves of steel, humans cannot survive deeper than just forty metres from the ocean's surface.

When it comes to what can survive down there, in perpetual darkness and crushing pressure, the story becomes even more incredible. Whales, the royalty of the deep, can dive to two thousand metres. The mystical giant squid lives at about one thousand metres. Most commonly known ocean fish remain above five hundred metres. Seals rarely dive deeper than one hundred metres. However, in the deepest trenches of the Earth's oceans, down to eight thousand metres, there exist creatures so bizarre that they seem fantastical. Vampire squids, giant sea spiders, gulper eels, bioluminescent lanternfish and jellyfish that create their own light to feed, survive and mate. Little is known about what lies even deeper, at the very bottom of the ocean, at eleven kilometres down. The mysteries of the deep, its secrets and its stories, are simply beyond reach and, for most, beyond their wildest imagination.

Such watery mysteries of the deep ocean were something that most people would rather not imagine at all, let alone see or experience. 'There's a good reason ancient cartographers drew sea monsters in the distant corners of their maps,' Laurence had once chuckled as Maddie and Tahu happily helped work his boat on an afternoon fishing expedition, beyond the reef shelf and past the drop-off. 'There is still so much we don't know; may never know...'

For Maddie though, the constancy, even the mystery of the deep, calmed and soothed her. It always had. Its secrets were its own. What was beneath her held her up. She knew that even when the surface became agitated, or worse – when it erupted in fury – its deep, silent core remained the same: ever-present and ever-powerful. 'It's not just still waters that run deep,' she reminded herself, 'but wild ones, too.'

Despite the warnings painted across the sky above, and lurking in the dark waters beneath, Maddie's contentment and surety in what she was doing endured. In that moment, with all its dangers and possibilities, she was as much in awe of the sea, in all its colours and its moods, as she had ever been.

Late in the afternoon now, *The Lady Jane* had been surfing along under spinnaker for nearly six hours, on a more south-easterly course to make better use of the now forty knot north-westerly. Now, with just fifty nautical miles to run to Norfolk, it was all 'starting to go pear-shaped', as Laurence would have said. Now, the spinnaker was down and tightly packed away, together with everything else that wasn't bolted down. Though not worried,

Maddie was certainly grim-faced. Her sloop was fighting its way to the peaks of now towering waves and diving, surfing, and crashing down the other side, only to bury its bow in the face of the next wave, as the weather relentlessly and mercilessly began to close in. She had reported her position two hours ago, along with her status – 'Running fast, storm sails set.' 'Eight bells and all's well!' Tahu would have remarked, as cool as he always was, when the ocean heaved and threatened to snarl. She had made her first direct radio contact with Norfolk Island just one hour ago and had passed her estimated time of arrival. Just five more hours of sailing. No, she had not required any assistance. Not then. Not at the time.

Now, for the first time, she wasn't so sure. It was raining heavily. The deck of *The Lady Jane* was constantly awash, and the cockpit drains were not coping with the deluge of water. The sun was once again setting, but this time behind a wall of water. Sea and rain merged into a gathering fury behind her. In the growing darkness, she could no longer see the massive waves coming at her from her port side. The wind lashed at her face, the raindrops stinging her like tiny bullets. The gusts were already well over fifty knots, and the waves were as many feet, probably more – she could no longer tell in the darkening maelstrom that she now knew was steadily consuming her.

She felt that she should be afraid. But she wasn't. Instead, she felt both a calmness and a determination that defied, maybe even challenged, this storm to do its worst. She would not falter. She was strong, and she would not fail.

The same could not be said for *The Lady Jane*. Even as Maddie shouted her defiance into the storm, the forward jib-line let go, the enormous strain on the line whipping it astern. Maddie felt the blow and instantly the sting of salt water in the wound that opened up on the right-hand side of her face. Both she and *The Lady Jane* staggered, as though punched by an unseen giant. As the foresail flung itself around the mast, the next wave hammered into the sloop and cascaded over her port side. *The Lady Jane* could not hold on. In a split second, she was rolled, and Maddie was thrown, still grimly gripping the wheel, into the churning sea.

Underwater, the noise of the storm became suddenly muted, though silent it was not. In its place, she could hear a wrenching and a screaming as her yacht was torn and twisted. Fibreglass sheeting was splintering. Aluminium supports, tortured beyond their limits, were succumbing to the overwhelming force of the waves. It was the most terrible sound she had ever heard.

Only for a moment though, for as suddenly as the storm had hurled the yacht over and plunged Maddie into the sea, it dragged them out again and upright, having rolled them through a full three hundred and sixty degrees. Still connected to *The Lady Jane* by her safety line, Maddie found herself hanging over the side rail, her legs still in the churning water, and her face jammed hard up against the hull of the sloop. The muted but terrible sounds of rendering steel and fibreglass were once again replaced by the howling wind and beating rain.

How long she hung there, she could not say. It could have been hours, but probably only minutes, before she managed to orientate herself and feel the adrenaline surge hot and fast through her battered body. She was having trouble seeing out of her right eye, but she could just make out the safety line and the rail beyond it. Reaching up with her left arm, she wrapped her fingers around the line and pulled hard. At the same time, she pushed against the hull with her right hip to free her right arm. As much as she willed it to move, her arm, savagely dislocated at the shoulder, hung limply by her side. Even through the adrenaline haze, the pain was terrible. But she knew she had to get back onto the boat, before the next wave. With a scream equal in determination as frustration, she pulled hard with her left arm and, scrambling with her feet, desperately tried to get some grip on the hull with her rubber shoes. As she did so, *The Lady Jane* shuddered and began to roll toward her. Maddie was plunged back into the water and, for a moment, submerged once more. This time her submersion was short-lived as *The Lady Jane* valiantly righted herself and Maddie found herself awkwardly straddling what remained of the safety rail.

Swinging her leg over the rail, she fell back into the stern – cold, hurt, and now afraid. Gasping and coughing, she peered forward through the driving rain at her yacht, or what was left of it. Lightning flashes revealed the devastation. The mast was gone, completely. The forward cabin roof was missing. What remained of the rigging was whipping around the deck in the howling wind. She struggled forward to the cabin, feeling her way. Mouthing a prayer of sorts, she located the emergency lighting panel and flicked the master switch on. Nothing.

"Come ON!" she shouted and flicked the switch off, then on again. This time – a response. The emergency lighting came on, feebly against the dark of the storm, but it was enough. And it was quite enough to reveal a gaping tear in the cabin floor, and in the hull beneath. *The Lady Jane* had not quite given up her keel, but the storm's attempt to wrench it from her had left a terrible wound, through which now the sea was pouring.

With her instincts and discipline returning, Maddie reached for the radio, which, almost unbelievably, seemed to be intact. Again, with a silent, pleading appeal, she raised the microphone to her lips.

"Mayday. Mayday. Mayday. This is The Lady Jane. This is The Lady Jane," she shouted over the roar of the wind. "I am disabled and taking water. My dead reckoning position is bearing two five zero degrees Norfolk Island at two five nautical miles."

Nothing.

"Please," she whispered. "Come on…"

But still nothing.

"Mayday. Mayday. Mayday…" She repeated her desperate transmission.

"Lady Jane, Lady Jane. This is The Pacific Quest. I read you, strength two. Say again your position."

"Oh, thank God!" she gasped as a wave of emotion swept over her. "Pacific Quest, Pacific Quest, I estimate my position at two five zero degrees Norfolk Island at two five miles. I am disabled. And injured. I require assistance."

The radio was quiet for what seemed like an eternity before it again crackled into life, this time scratchy and barely readable.

"Lady Jane, Lady Jane, this is The Pacific Quest. My position.... southeast...... miles.... far.... away......"

There was a long pause and a lot of static. "I want to help you..." Then, even more static. "But I cannot reach you.... I just cannot reach you."

And the voice, so strong at first, was gone. The radio was silent.

The storm, however, was not. The screaming of the wind went on unabated, and although the lightning and thunder continued to assault the night, the driving rain seemed to have eased. Crippled and effectively keel-less, *The Lady Jane* wallowed and staggered with each surge of each wave. Although the emergency power was still running one of her two pumps, the sloop was steadily taking water, and was slowly settling in the heaving and agitated sea.

Maddie knew that her boat was dying. She could not save her. All she could do was save herself. Her life raft, firmly attached to the front deck, had remarkably survived the violent roll and now, too, was to be tested by the night and the storm. Abandoning the radio, Maddie inched her way forward to the raft. She would allow the rising waters to lift her off the deck rather than risk a launch off the side of the sloop whilst it was still afloat. She knew that that was the best way. But with her right arm useless and almost crippling her with pain, and as good as blind in her right eye, deep down she felt a sudden tightening in her bowels and a furious pounding of her heart. She was beginning to panic.

Somehow, she managed to clamber into the raft and release all but one of the bindings, which she would release as the waters began to float her off the stricken yacht. Enclosed in the canvas raft, she felt strangely secure, and from somewhere deep inside of her she could feel herself lifting in hope; in the belief that she could, and would, make it. She was now more composed, and even as the storm continued to assault her, her earlier sense of surreal calm was returning.

She spent the next hour, she thought, inside the raft, on top of her sinking sloop. But the end was drawing near. With *The Lady Jane* almost fully submerged beneath her, Maddie released the final binding and was instantly swept off the sinking deck.

3

Exhaustion exacts a particular toll. When she awoke, Maddie took some time to realise where she was and what had happened. Her flimsy craft was secure and, incredibly, still reasonably dry inside. The raft's survival beacon still seemed to be operating, and outside, the sky, although still leaden, was glowing a soft pink with dawn's first light. The swell was still significant, and the rolling wave tops still towered over her. But she was alive. She had come through the night and the storm.

The long and deep horn blast was so unexpected that for some minutes Maddie did not react at all. Drifting in and out of consciousness, she had to tell herself that this was real; that somehow, she had been found, and she still had to assist whomever it was in the large white vessel that was now rapidly looming out of the east. She unzipped the roof of the raft and, once again, the icy wind stung as it cut through her. But she could do little more. Now, with rescue seemingly imminent, she had little left.

The white vessel eased alongside her, both craft pitching up and down with the swell. As if from a great distance, she could hear people calling to her, calling to each other, and calling her name. Her vision blurred with fatigue, and with tears, she saw arms reach towards her and felt strong hands take hold of her. Blinking hard and gasping, as the spray lashed and stung her face, she looked up and peered into the face of her rescuer. There was no mistaking the eyes and the smile of Tahu Taleka.

"It's okay, Maddie. I've got you! I've got you! You're going to be all right. We're taking you back to Norfolk. We're taking you home."

And suddenly, there were other voices, and other hands gently carrying her, and even more gently laying her down. She felt powerful engines growl into life and the vessel surge forward. But she remembered nothing else.

4

Norfolk Island is one of the most dramatically beautiful places on Earth. Not a tropical paradise – its latitude takes care of that – but a paradise, nevertheless. Emboldened for seven-eighths of its girth by towering cliffs, it is also a fortress. To assail it from the sea presents challenges beyond the capacity of most. Those who come to this place are, without exception, in awe of it.

Norfolk Island is steeped in a history that almost beggars belief. To walk the ruins of Kingston and to pause in its quietest corners, one can still hear the screams of agony and helplessness pouring from the throats of the convict wretches who were condemned there. And yet, to stand on top of Mount Pitt and breathe the salt air, absorbing the stunning beauty of the island 'given' to the descendants of the mutineers who had wrenched the Bounty from its captain, William Bligh, to set him adrift in a long boat, to themselves flee to tiny Pitcairn Island – only to be pardoned decades later and allowed this paradise – one cannot help but be entranced. It is truly an amazing place.

To be born on Norfolk is to share an extraordinary heritage with a people quietly but fiercely proud of their past, and of 'their island'. To visit Norfolk is to be given a rare glimpse of that heritage; to witness it, to continue it. Those who know Norfolk love her. Those who belong there know it. To find Norfolk is to find yourself.

Laurence James Clay found that elusive peace when he was just thirty years young, a qualified and dedicated meteorologist, a lover of the sea, and all it brings. His business, his science, and his art was interpreting her actions and predicting her moods. He was competent. He was content. But he was not complete. Norfolk Island brought him what he lacked. It brought him peace. And ironically, only by leaving for a time, did it bring him more than he could ever have dreamed of – a son.

Laurence had known Madeline Spencer Christian all her life. He regarded her as part of his family, and he knew, particularly after her own father's passing, that he was an integral part of hers. He had taught her all he knew about the sea. He had tried, anyway. A bright and intuitive sailor, she had, however, a relentless determination and sometimes-stubborn independence about her that would occasionally frustrate him. Tahu helped change all that. Even as children, Tahu had a way with her that calmed her and brought out the very best in her. They were inseparable, and he loved them both. He often felt that what he could not teach Maddie, Tahu could.

Grim-faced and tired, Laurence stared for some time out to sea in the direction they had come from the morning before, still quietly cursing that they had not been able to make better speed through the mountainous seas they had faced the previous night, when they responded to the garbled Mayday call from *The Lady Jane*. They had not been able to make contact with Maddie, but could hear her frightened exchange with another vessel, although they could not hear its transmissions, nor make out its name. He sighed and turned to walk inside. Though he knew and loved the sea, he also knew that at times she could be most unforgiving.

"So, you're awake today!" he said brightly as he walked into Maddie's room. "Anybody would think that you've had a hard time of it lately."

"Laurence!" Maddie smiled, then winced. She gently touched the right-hand side of her face, lightly brushing over the stitches that ran from her ear down to the back of her jaw.

"Just ten or so, they tell me," Laurence grinned. "You'll hardly notice them!"

She held out her hand, which he took in both of his. "Laurence," she said again. "What do I say?"

"You gave us quite a fright, Maddie. We knew you were coming but weren't expecting such a dramatic arrival. You certainly know how to make a homecoming! We thought we were going to lose our newest doctor before she arrived, let alone opened for business."

"That sounds nice, Laurence. Home! I feel like I am home."

"The way it should be. Welcome home." and he patted her hand.

"Thank you, Laurence. I'm sorry to have made such an entrance. Just like old times, eh, you saving my behind!" She smiled again, then paused, looking past Laurence towards the door.

"Is, umm… Is Tahu here? May I see him?"

"Tahu?"

"Of course! I had been hoping so much that he might still be around here, and then… there he was! I was never so pleased to see anyone in my entire life. I can't wait to see him!"

"Maddie…"

"I know that it's been a long time. I've been missing. Probably in more ways than I like to admit. But let me tell you, my little heart skipped a beat when I saw him reaching out to me!"

"Maddie, what are you talking about?"

"When Tahu plucked me out of the raft…"

"Maddie," Laurence said slowly. "I pulled you from the sea, not Tahu."

"No, I'm sure it was Tahu. I know it's been a few years, but I couldn't mistake those beautiful eyes."

"Maddie," Laurence said again, more firmly. "It wasn't Tahu. It was me."

"But Laurence…"

"Maddie!" There was a hint of strain, almost a crack in his voice.

"Laurence, I saw him. He called to me."

"Maddie, please! You don't understand." He turned and walked to the window, where he stood for some time staring far out to sea.

"Maddie…" he said eventually, with measure and control back in his voice, "You've been gone a long time. Much has changed around here." Again, he was silent as he continued to stare out the window.

Then, with a sigh, he turned and looked directly at her.

"Maddie… Tahu is dead. He was lost at sea. Two years ago. A terrible storm. His ship went down off Nuku'alofa. There were only three survivors. The sea took the rest. Maddie… dearest Maddie… Tahu is gone…" His voice broke. His pale blue eyes brimmed with tears, and his lips trembled. He swallowed hard and took a deep breath. He ran his hand through his thick grey hair.

"Maddie, Tahu did not pull you from the sea. He was not with us when we found you. He has not been with us for so long that… that… it already seems like forever. And… and I miss him so very much." Tears were running down the old man's weathered cheeks as he took another deep breath. "I am so sorry Maddie…. We tried to find you."

Maddie did not remember Laurence leaving the room. Everything was spinning around her. She couldn't focus. She couldn't speak. For a moment, she felt that she couldn't even breathe. She felt an enormous weight on her chest and a ringing in her ears. She could feel her pulse pounding in her temples and her throat constricting. She knew she was sobbing, but she was so numb, so detached from where she was and what she was trying to understand, that she could not feel her body shaking. Later, she recalled thinking for a second that she should wake up now, that everything would be all right, as it should be, as it was before – as she so desperately wanted it to be.

When she did awake, it was late afternoon. The shadows were different, and the light softer. Feeling remarkably and surprisingly better, she got up, put on a dressing gown and slippers, and opened the outside door to her room. She gratefully filled her lungs with the mild afternoon sea air, then made her way slowly to the end of the lawn.

The hospital garden was bordered with roses, and their gentle fragrance was welcome. Down green hillsides, and perched on the edge of the cliffs, the Norfolk Island pine trees stood tall, their sparse but strong branches held out majestically into the sea breeze. Along the rocky base of the cliffs, the waters of Sydney Bay rhythmically washed the island's shoreline. Beyond the cliffs and the wide sweeping bay they embraced, the deeper waters of the Strait flexed their muscle. Across the strait, and defiant as ever, lay Phillip Island. Its striking barren slopes rose abruptly from the sea, catching the late afternoon sun and glowing like the ruins of an ancient, forbidden temple. Beyond the island, and beyond its foreboding presence, the vast blue and green waters of the South Pacific Ocean stretched out to an infinite horizon. Blue and green. The colours of the sea. She closed her eyes and breathed deeply.

She looked back towards Phillip Island and the rolling, churning waters of the strait. All at once powerful, immeasurable, and terrifying. Yet, deeply calming, inviting, and sure. Again, her thoughts turned to Tahu. Even now, she was sure that it was Tahu who had reached out to her, who had called her name. His hands had plucked her from the sea. His eyes had looked into hers and given her the strength to survive. She knew his eyes. She knew his voice. It could have been no other. But it wasn't him. He was not there. In her distress and in her desire, she had simply imagined it.

She must have been standing there for some time, because before she realised, she was watching the sun sink graciously into the western horizon, into the vast indigo expanse of the South Pacific. A fiery orange glow lit up the tops of the waves. Leaden clouds at the horizon were splashed with streaks of vivid scarlet. Clinging to the last vestiges of blue sky and capturing the very last of the sun's rays, those higher up hung suspended in soft shrouds of delicate pink. The end of a day. But the promise of another.

Without looking, she knew that Laurence was standing behind her.

"Y'okay, Maddie?" There was great warmth in his words.

"U'huh," she murmured, reaching behind her for his great weathered hands.

"Nice to have you back, Maddie," and he gently squeezed her hand.

They stood in silence for some time. There was no hurry. There was not much to say. They both knew that. And that was okay.

"Laurence...?"

"Yes, Maddie?"

"I am so sorry about Tahu. If I'd known, I would have… I'd……"

"It's okay, Maddie. I know."

Above them, a pair of white terns, in perfect harmony, hovered gracefully in the onshore breeze, their elegant, snow-white wings fully outstretched, their plaintive cry familiar and comforting.

"Laurence…" She paused, searching. "He was special, your Tahu. We were …um…. He and I… we were …" Her voice trailed off, her throat suddenly tight.

Long had she wondered about their reunion. Even yesterday, she had held hope that somehow he had waited for her – that somehow he would rescue her from the world that had enticed her, and yes, had rewarded her. But now he was gone. And not just gone. Gone for two years.

"Oh, Tahu…" she whispered, keenly aware of how arrogant she had been to even imagine that he would still be interested in rescuing her from anything, least of all from herself.

And yet, ironically, in his place, the only one who had been prepared to risk so much for her was his father. And that distant sailor. 'Lady Jane, Lady Jane. This is The Pacific Quest. I want to help you.' The scratchy words were there again. 'But I cannot reach you!'

She wondered about the sailor who made that call. He knew that Maddie was in desperate trouble. She sensed, in his reply, that he also knew her fear. There was something about his urgency. Something familiar. Almost personal. The sea is like that though. All-encompassing. Never judgemental. She quietly thanked him for answering her call. He knew that in the void of fear, words, any words, were sword and shield. Whoever he was, he knew the sea, and he knew those who knew the sea. And she was grateful.

The breeze was cooler now, and she shivered. The sea seemed almost black, a deep ebony, barely distinguishable from the night sky. The colours of the sea – veiled by the coming of night. Yet, the distant roll of the surf against Kingston beach bore witness to its continuous watch over the island. Unseen, but constant, and sure.

Yes, Tahu was right. In so many ways, she now realised that he had indeed rescued her. Just not the way she had imagined. Though their friendship seemed so long ago, what he had given her was priceless, beyond compare. He had given her perspective. He had given her hope. Eventually, you have to return to where you started from. Eventually, you have to come 'home', to know just how far you have come, to know who you have become. And to be 'okay' with all of that.

And she knew.

"Laurence?"

"Yes, Maddie."

"What was the name of the ship Tahu was on?"

"A research ship, Maddie. Out of Auckland. She was called The Pacific Quest. Why, Maddie?"

———

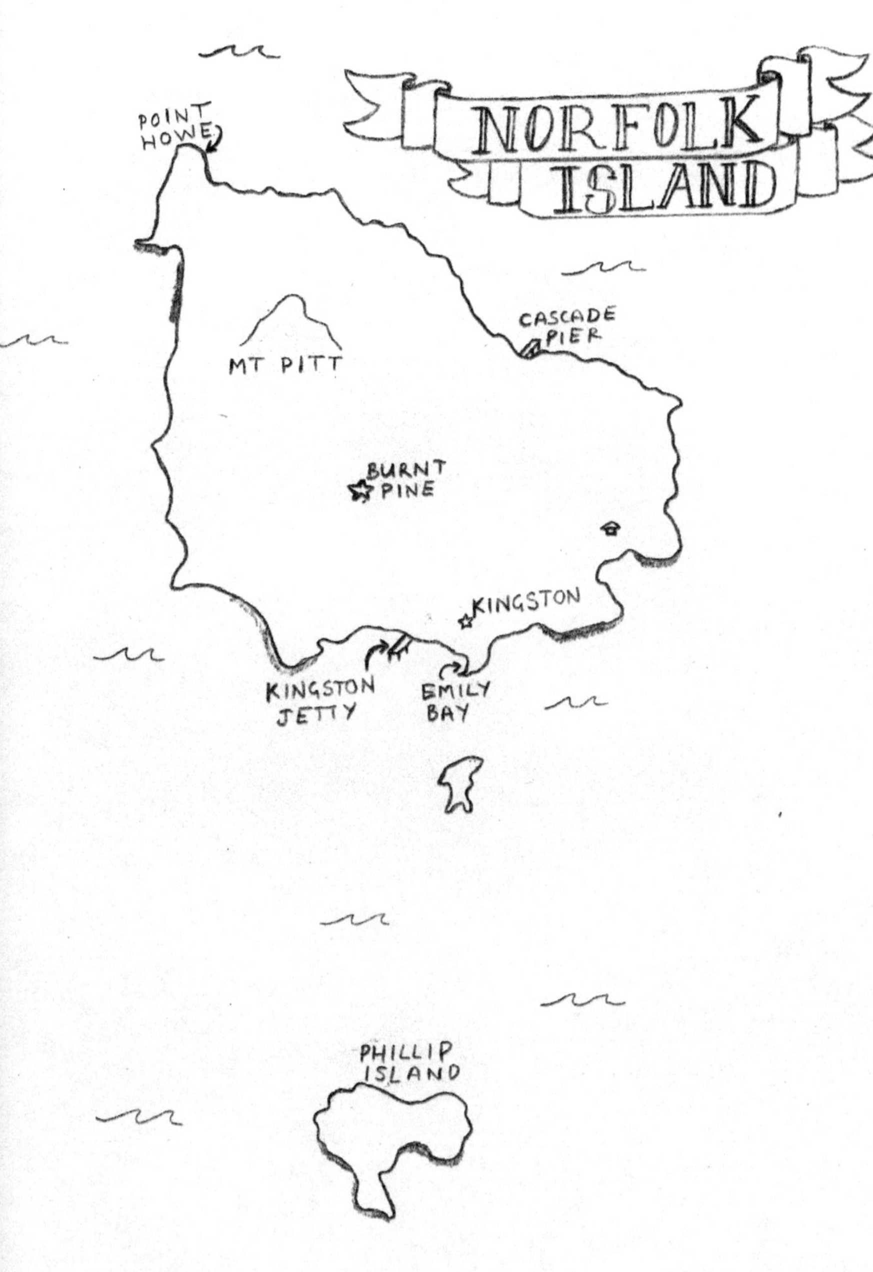

NORFOLK ISLAND
POINT HOWE
CASCADE PIER
MT PITT
BURNT PINE
KINGSTON
KINGSTON JETTY
EMILY BAY
PHILLIP ISLAND

The Author: Guy Hall

Guy was born in Melbourne but, as the son of a soldier, grew up in various places in Australia and the United States of America.

He joined the Royal Australian Air Force in 1980 and flew as an operational pilot and Flying Instructor until 1990, when he joined Australian Airlines and then Qantas Airways in 1994.

Guy also has a degree in Science (Physics) from The University of Melbourne. Seeing the world through a pilot's and a scientist's eyes, however, has not prevented him from often standing agape (his words) at the extraordinary, the beautiful, and the seemingly perfect design of the planet.

Now retired from flying, he and his wife Jo-anne share their time between homes on Norfolk Island and Melbourne, where their five children, and growing numbers of grandchildren, live, work, grow and play.

Guy and Jo-anne's time in Norfolk Island has also reignited his long-standing passion for writing. Guy will happily tell you that he is a better writer when 'on island'. Inspired by this remote South Pacific Island, its astonishing natural beauty, and its timeless story, Guy has named his independent publishing company 'Tiny Fish Publishing'.

ABOUT US.

The Illustrator: Meredith Hall

Meredith lives in Melbourne, Australia. She trained as a Fashion Designer, where hand drawing remains a key skill. Her preferred medium is pencil, as it allows her to capture mood as well as fine detail. Following on from her acclaimed illustration of *Our Vietnam* (Tiny Fish Publishing 2025), Meredith has continued her partnership with Guy to illustrate his *Colours of the Sea* series of novellas, centred on Norfolk Island.